TRIPLET TROUBLE
and
the Field Day Disaster

There are more books about
the Tucker Triplets!

Triplet Trouble and the Talent Show Mess

Triplet Trouble and the Runaway Reindeer

Triplet Trouble and the Red Heart Race

TRIPLET TROUBLE
and
the Field Day Disaster

by Debbie Dadey and Marcia Thornton Jones
Illustrated by John Speirs

A
LITTLE APPLE
PAPERBACK

SCHOLASTIC INC.
New York Toronto London Auckland Sydney

No part of this publication may be reproduced in whole or in part, or stored in a retrieval system, or transmitted in any form or by any means, electronic, mechanical, photocopying, recording, or otherwise, without written permission of the publisher. For information regarding permission, write to Scholastic Inc., 555 Broadway, New York, NY 10012.

ISBN 0-590-58107-4

12 11 10   3 4 5 6 7 8 9/0

Printed in the U.S.A.   40

First Scholastic printing, May 1996

To Barbara and Lee Beckham — who truly understand my enthusiasm for sports!

—MTJ

To Crystal and Heidi Ptacek

—DD

Contents

1. Ready for Trouble   1

2. Practice   6

3. Dad   13

4. Team Plan   19

5. Field Day Trouble   25

6. Field Day Fool   33

7. Three Legs   40

8. Who's the Best?   46

TRIPLET TROUBLE
and
the Field Day Disaster

1

Ready for Trouble

Mr. Parker wrote in big letters on a piece of paper. All of the second-graders in my class held their breaths. Whenever Mr. Parker made a sign it usually meant more work.

We didn't want more work. Especially me. My name is Sam Johnson. I'm not the best soccer player in the second grade, but

I still couldn't wait for the weekend. It was a warm spring Friday afternoon. Perfect weather for soccer. I hoped Mr. Parker wasn't going to give more homework.

Mr. Parker held up his new sign. In bright pink letters it said: FIELD DAY MONDAY.

Ashley Tucker hopped out of her seat. "Spending the day in a field with cows and

horses sounds like a great idea," she said.

Adam Tucker shook his head. Adam is Ashley's brother. He is very smart. "Field Day is a sports day," he told her. "We get to compete in all kinds of games."

"I hope our class wins," Alex Tucker said. "Mr. Parker would be proud. It would be terribly perfect!"

"With me on the team, we'll win for sure," Adam said. "I'm the fastest runner in Mr. Parker's class."

"What do you mean?" Alex asked.

Adam puffed out his chest. "I'll be the Field Day champion. Everybody knows I'm the best athlete in the class."

Ashley giggled. Ashley giggles a lot. "No, you're not," she said. "I am."

"You're both wrong," Alex told them. "I'm better than both of you put together."

Ashley, Adam, and Alex are triplets. They all have the same birthday, and they even look like each other. But they never seem to agree on anything.

Alex's eyes got big and round. Then she snapped her fingers right in front of her nose. That could only mean one thing. Alex had another one of her brilliant ideas.

"We'll practice all weekend," she said. "Then we'll *all* be the best!"

Sometimes I like Alex's ideas. But not today. I sighed. It didn't look like I was going to play soccer this weekend.

2

Practice

"I thought we were going to play soccer this weekend," I said. The triplets and I were walking home from school.

"We have to practice for Field Day this weekend," Alex said.

"Alex is right," Ashley said. "Field Day is more important."

"I have to walk Cleo," I told them.

Alex grinned. "Bring Cleo to our house. She can help us practice."

I wasn't sure that was a good idea. Cleo is the best dog in the world but whenever she gets near the Tucker Triplets, there's always trouble. But I hurried home and got Cleo anyway.

The triplets were waiting for me in their yard. Cleo jumped up and licked Alex on her nose. Then Cleo ran to Adam and Ashley. Adam scratched her floppy ears. Ashley sneezed. Ashley always sneezes when Cleo's around.

"We need a cheer," Ashley said.

Adam puffed out his chest. "You can cheer for me."

"We should cheer for the class," I said.

"I know the perfect cheer," Ashley said.

Ashley moved her arms in crazy circles and started to yell.

Who's the best?
We're the best!
Better than all the rest!

Then Ashley screamed so loud Cleo whined and hid behind me.

"We won't be the best unless we practice," Alex said. She picked up her jump rope

and made a big loop out of it. "We'll practice lassoing," she said. Then she dropped the jump rope loop over Cleo's head.

Cleo looked up at me with her big brown eyes. I bent down and pulled the jump rope off Cleo. "We don't need to know how to lasso," I told Alex.

"Lassoing is a perfectly good contest for Field Day," Alex argued.

Adam laughed at his sister. "We need to know how to win races."

"Let's practice running," I said before Alex could argue.

We all lined up. Adam said go. Then we headed across the Tuckers' backyard as fast as we could go. So did Cleo. Only Cleo didn't run in a straight line. She ran circles around us and barked.

When we didn't stop, Cleo reached up and grabbed Adam's shorts in her teeth. Adam fell down. I stopped to pull Cleo away from Adam. Alex laughed so hard, she sat down in the middle of the yard. Ashley raced across the finish line first and started cheering.

Adam didn't like to be laughed at. Adam's face was red. He glared at Cleo.

"I think we practiced enough," I said and grabbed Cleo's collar.

Alex laughed. "Adam is sure to win the grass eating contest!"

Who's the best?
We're the best!
Better than all the rest!

I heard Ashley cheering as Cleo and I walked home. I wasn't so sure she was right. We needed a lot more practice before we were the best. Saturday was going to be a terribly long day.

3

Dad

The next morning was Saturday. At breakfast, I told my dad about Field Day. He was very excited. "Sam," he told me. "I used to be the fastest member of my relay team."

"Relay team?" I asked, finishing my last bit of cereal.

"Sure," Dad told me. "Come outside and I'll show you."

Cleo, Dad, and I went out in the front yard. In two minutes, Alex, Ashley, and Adam were in my front yard, too. The triplets always seem to show up when my dad and I are in the yard.

"Hi!" Alex said. She smiled so big she showed the space where her front tooth used to be.

"I was showing Sam how to run a relay race," Dad told them. "You're just in time to help."

"Is Cleo in the race?" Alex asked, hugging Cleo around the neck.

Dad laughed. "I think she'll just watch this time." Dad looked at Cleo and said in a stern voice, "Cleo, stay." Cleo sat

14

down and watched us. I knew Cleo would stay. She always minds Dad.

Adam looked at Cleo. I knew he was glad Cleo wouldn't be tripping him today. Ashley looked at Cleo and sneezed.

In just a few minutes, Dad had us running around the yard. We took turns handing a stick to each other, just like a

real relay race. It was fun, almost as much fun as soccer.

Dad went into the house and we sat on the porch. "We should wear blue T-shirts on Monday," Ashley told us, "since it's our school color."

"I was going to wear my lucky red baseball shirt," Adam told her.

"It doesn't matter what color we wear," Alex told her.

"Yes, it does," Ashley said. "We should definitely wear blue. Right, Sam?"

I looked at Ashley. Ashley is terribly perfect about doing the right thing. If I said yes to her, Adam and Alex would be terribly mad at me. There was only one thing to do.

"Come on, Cleo," I yelled. "Let's go for a walk!"

4

Team Plan

On Monday morning I headed to the Tuckers' house. The Tuckers live on the same street as me. We always walk to school together.

I hopped over a roller skate and jogged around a wagon with a missing wheel to get to the Tuckers' front door. Alex opened the door. I guess the triplets agreed to wear our school's color. But Alex hates to look like everyone else. She always tries to be different. Today, she had on blue shorts and a blue straw hat. A blue bandana was tied around her neck. She even wore blue cowboy boots.

"Why are you dressed like that?" I asked. I was wearing blue soccer shorts, my lucky blue baseball cap, a blue t-shirt and tennis shoes.

When Alex smiled she showed the space where her front tooth used to be. "Mr. Parker said to be ready to spend a day in the field," she said.

"But he meant the soccer field," I told her. "You can't win a relay race wearing cowboy boots."

"Yes, I can," Alex said. "I'm so fast, it doesn't matter what I wear on my feet. And I can definitely win a roping contest." She held up her jump rope. She had it knotted in a loop. I was glad Cleo wasn't there.

Adam and Ashley pushed their way past Alex. "I wish we had more time to practice," Ashley said. "Look, I made a sign." Ashley held up her sign.

"Let's go," Adam said. "I'm ready to win my blue ribbons. I'd be great even if we hadn't practiced at all."

"It doesn't matter how good you are," Ashley reminded him. "We're supposed to compete as a class."

"Well, I have the perfect team plan," Alex said. "Stay out of my way and I'll be the champ. Then our team will win, too."

"No, you won't. I'll be the champ," Adam said.

Alex dropped her jump rope lasso over Adam's shoulders. "I'm going to be the champ," she said.

Adam wiggled out of the lasso and stomped down the sidewalk without answering his sister. I liked Adam and I liked Alex. But when they fought over who was best, there was bound to be trouble.

5

Field Day Trouble

When we got on the field, Mr. Parker held up a big sign. In green letters it said: FIRST EVENT JUMPING CONTEST.

Adam puffed out his chest. "Let me go first."

Our class lined up next to the second grade class from Lincoln School. Adam ran up to the chalk line. Then he jumped

a long way. "I knew I could jump farther than anybody," Adam said.

Ashley started to cheer.

Who's the best?
We're the best!
Better than all the rest!

Everyone cheered with her. Everyone but Alex. When it was Alex's turn to jump her cowboy boots slid out from under her. Down went Alex. I tried not to laugh.

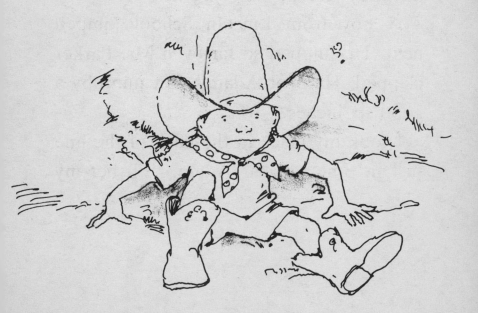

"Don't worry," I told Alex. "We all get two chances."

Alex stuck out her lower lip and stomped to the end of the line. I couldn't worry about Alex now because it was my turn to jump.

I ran as fast as I could until I reached the chalk line on the grass. Then I sailed through the air. I swung my arms hoping they would help me fly farther than anybody else. It didn't work.

A boy from Lincoln School jumped next. He jumped so far even Mr. Parker clapped. He beat Adam's first jump by a good six inches.

I took my place in the back of the line just in time to hear Adam. "I'll bet my

next jump beats that boy's," he said. "I'll set the school record."

"You shouldn't brag so much," Barbara told him.

Maria nodded. "We don't care about you and your records."

When everybody near Adam muttered that Maria was right, Alex's eyes got big. Then she snapped her fingers right in front of her nose. I knew that look. It meant Alex was thinking up another one of her ideas. Today, I knew it meant trouble. Field Day trouble. I was right.

Alex leaned over and whispered to Ashley.

Ashley giggled and bent down to tie her sneakers good and tight. But that's not all she did. She tugged on Adam's shoelace. He didn't notice. He was too busy arguing with Maria.

When it was Adam's turn to try his second jump Alex gave him a little push.

"Go ahead," Alex told Adam. "Break the record!"

Adam puffed out his chest. "Watch this," he told everybody. Then he took a running start. Just as he reached the chalk line, his shoe fell off. Adam gave a little hop. It was the shortest jump of the day.

Lincoln School hooted for the other class. "We won!" they cheered. Nobody from our team cheered. We all looked at Adam and frowned. Adam glared at his sisters. With the Tucker Triplets around, Field Day was a terrible mess!

6

Field Day Fool

Adam is the smartest kid in Mr. Parker's room. He is also the best pitcher and catcher. That's why I was glad the next event was the egg throwing contest. I was sure we'd win with him on our team.

Mr. Parker waited until we were lined up across from our partners.

33

Alex threw the egg to me and I caught it. I jumped up and down; I was so happy. Then I threw the egg to Alex. The egg landed right on top of her cowboy hat. SPLAT!

Barbara threw her egg next. Randy had to lean way over to catch it. We cheered when he held up the egg. Then he tossed it back to Barbara. When she tried to grab it, the egg slipped through her fingers. She looked like she was juggling when she tried to catch it in her other hand. The second-

graders from Lincoln Elementary School laughed when it landed on top of her sneaker. Even Mr. Parker smiled.

Nobody else in our class did any better until it was Adam and Ashley's turn. Adam threw the egg perfectly. Ashley caught it and jumped up and down.

"Thank goodness," Ashley said with a giggle. Ashley hates to get dirty.

"Just throw it," Adam told her. "I'm the best catcher here. I can catch anything you throw."

Ashley nodded her head, closed her eyes, and threw the egg. SPLAT! The egg landed right on Adam's forehead. Slimy yolk ran down his face.

Everyone on the field laughed. Adam didn't laugh. He yelled at Ashley. "Why did you throw it so hard?"

Ashley shrugged her shoulders. "You said you could catch whatever I threw."

Adam's face was red under the egg. "I didn't think you were going to blast the egg into orbit!"

Alex laughed even harder. "An eggstronaut!" she yelled.

Adam stomped off to wash his face. Adam hates to lose. But he hates being teased even worse. I knew he felt like a Field Day Fool.

I didn't feel so good myself. There were only two more events left and our team was way behind. The day was turning into a disaster. A Field Day Disaster!

7

Three Legs

"This is terrible," Ashley complained. "Lincoln School is beating the pants off us."

Adam smiled. "Don't worry. I know I can win the three-legged race. Especially if I have a good partner."

Adam looked right at me and winked. I hoped we would be partners, too.

Mr. Parker called out names from our
class. Adam stomped his foot when I got
Ashley for a partner and he got Alex.

"Don't worry," I told Adam. "Alex is
a fast runner, too."

Alex is a fast runner, but not when she's wearing cowboy boots. Instead of crossing the finish line first, Adam and Alex ended up in a big pile on the ground. One of Alex's boots landed on Adam's head.

Ashley and I ran past them, but we weren't fast enough. Two kids from Lincoln School beat us. They started their own cheer.

We're number one!
The best under the sun!
Forget all the rest,
Because we're the best!

"Hey!" Ashley yelled. "That's not fair. Our cheer says we're the best."

"We've lost all three events so far," Adam said sadly. "They ARE the best."

Alex threw her cowboy hat on the ground. "We can't give up," she said. "Field Day isn't over."

Adam shook his head. "I haven't won anything."

Ashley put her hands on her hips. "You're right. But we can't give up."

I put my hand on Adam's shoulder. "The last event is the tug-of-war. Maybe if we all work together, we can be the Field Day champs."

Adam smiled. "I know just what to do. I need to be in front."

Alex shook her head. "You and Sam should be in the back and I'll be in the front."

"That's not right," Ashley said. "I have to . . ."

I didn't listen to what Ashley said. Winning the tug-of-war looked hopeless.

8

Who's the Best?

Mr. Parker held up a new sign. The bright purple letters said: LAST EVENT TUG-OF-WAR.

The second-graders from Lincoln School lined up on the left. Mr. Parker's class lined up on the right. Everybody, that is, except Adam, Ashley, and Alex. They were too busy being mad at each other.

Mr. Parker blew his whistle and both teams grabbed the fat rope.

"Pull!" Randy shouted.

I pulled as hard as I could. So did everyone else. But the second-graders from Lincoln School pulled harder. Our team was being pulled straight toward the white chalk line drawn between our two teams.

I dug my heels into the ground, but that didn't work. Our team was going to lose.

Just then, Adam started cheering louder than everybody else.

We can win when
We work as a team!

We all started cheering with him when Adam picked up the end of the rope. Then Ashley and Alex grabbed the rope, too. Alex dug her boots into the dirt. The more we cheered, the harder we pulled. Slowly, we pulled the Lincoln second-graders closer and closer to the chalk line.

We gave a final tug, pulling the Lincoln team across the line. They landed in a big heap.

"Who's the best?" Mr. Parker yelled.

"We're the best!" we all cheered back.

"So let out a scream!" Ashley yelled.

And we did. Thanks to the Tucker Triplets, Mr. Parker's second-graders were the Tug-of-War Champs!

Sometimes having the Tucker Triplets in Mr. Parker's class is trouble, but sometimes it's terribly terrific!

Creepy, weird, wacky and
funny things happen to
the Bailey School Kids!™
Collect and read them all!

The Adventures of THE BAILEY SCHOOL KIDS®

The Adventures of
THE
BAILEY SCHOOL
KIDS™

He always appears wrapped up
in bandages. He doesn't know anything
about softball. Could the new softball
coach really be a *mummy*?

If Liza, Melody, Eddie and Howie
don't find out soon, the Bailey Batters
may never win another game!

The Adventures of The Bailey School Kids #21

Mummies Don't Coach Softball

by Debbie Dadey and Marcia Thorton Jones

Sliding into a bookstore near you.

BSKT1095